This edition ©Ward Lock Limited 1989

First published in the United States
in 1990 by Gallery Books,
an imprint of W.H. Smith Publishers, Inc.,
112 Madison Avenue, New York 10016.

Gallery Books are available for bulk purchase for sales
promotions and premium use. For details write or telephone
the Manager of Special Sales, W.H. Smith Publishers, Inc.,
112 Madison Avenue, New York, New York 10016. (212) 532-6600.

ISBN 0-8317-0967-7

Printed and bound in Hungary

THE RABBITS' NEW HOME

GALLERY BOOKS
An Imprint of W. H. Smith Publishers Inc
112 Madison Avenue
New York, New York 10016

"Why can't *we* go to Brambledown?"

Chapter One

MIDDLEMARSH

In a little spot south of North and north of South lies Brambledown. Do you know it? If you do, you know that there is no finer place to live.

Oh, it has its squabbles and it has its sulks. It has its bullies and it has its bad-guys. But for the most part, the little creatures who live in and around the village of Brambledown are as happy as can be. People say far and wide, "How lovely it must be to live in Brambledown! Such friendly people *and* a wonderful market in Farmer Hayseed's garden."

Even the Brown rabbit family, living far off in Middlemarsh, had heard nothing but good about Brambledown.

"Why can't we go to live there?" said little Blondie, looking longingly across the fields.

"Nonsense, child!" said her father, Barney Brown. "We have a perfectly good home here in Middlemarsh. I have lived in this burrow since I was born. Now please will you all pull in your elbows and squeeze up while Ma chops the carrots for dinner."

So everybody huddled closer together and tucked in their paws and pulled in their elbows and ears while Mrs Brown chopped the carrots for dinner. Because, you see, the burrow was very small and there was hardly room for a pair of elbows to bend unless everyone curled up small.

Barney Brown's family was getting bigger all the time. The bigger the family grew, the smaller the burrow seemed to be. Barney had to sleep out in the open – even in the winter.

"You should find a bigger house," said Mrs Mouse.

"Find a bigger house"

She had gone by one morning and seen Barney all dripping wet from sleeping out in the rain.

"Nonsense," said Barney. "This is the burrow where I was born. There's nothing wrong with it."

Barney, all dripping wet

That was not quite true. Not only was the Brown's house rather small, but the rain dribbled in around the door. A railway ran close by, too, and the trains made an awful din and shook the burrow till earth tumbled down on the rabbits inside and the walls began to bulge. It was quite scary.

"Why don't we go to live in Brambledown?" said little Blondie.

"Nonsense," said Barney. "I've already told you once, we have a perfectly good house right here . . . Hold tight everybody! I hear another train coming!"

Then one morning Mr Mole came knocking at the door. "Make room! Make room!" he said, barging into the burrow. "People from the big town are building a road across Marsh Meadow. Lots of animals have lost their homes. Everybody in Middlemarsh must make room for the home-less ones!"

"Make room! Make room!"

"Take it! Why not take the whole burrow! Take it all!" said Barney Brown, stamping his foot angrily. "We were going anyway."

"*Going*, dear?" asked Mrs Brown.

"To Brambledown?" asked Blondie.

"I regret to say," said Barney solemnly, "that I do not know *exactly* the way to Brambledown. But we shall find something . . . somewhere . . . somehow."

So Mr and Mrs Brown loaded all their babies – Baxter and Boris and Blondie and Billie and Bud – into a barrow and they left the burrow in Middlemarsh. And the rain rained in and the trains went thundering by, but Mr Mole was just glad to have a roof over his head and a place for the homeless ones.

All night they travelled, through rain and driving wind. Curled up in the barrow, the little rabbits fell fast asleep. So they did not see the orchards or the river or the pond or any of the route Barney took. They simply woke up next morning to find themselves beside a little green door at the foot of a tall elm tree. The sun was shining, and a sign on the door said: TO LET.

First Barney, then his wife Bea, and then each little rabbit in turn peeped inside.

"It's brilliant," said Barney.

"It's beautiful," said Bea.

"It's so BIG," said Baxter and Boris and Blondie and Billie and Bud.

"Run away and play till suppertime"

Chapter Two

A STRANGE NEW LAND

There was a pretty view through the trees and across the fields to a little village with red rooftops. "I wonder where we are," said Barney. "Wherever it is, I think it will suit us very well."

"I *did* want to live in Brambledown," said Blondie. "People say it's so fine."

"Well this is fine, too," said her brother. "What could be finer?"

". . . as big as a barn," said Barney.

". . . as dry as a bone," said Boris.

". . . as cosy as a cuddle," said Bud.

"Baxter and Boris, you help me unload the barrow. You youngest children run away and play till suppertime," said Mrs Brown, "but don't go far, mind! Remember you are in a strange new place now. You don't know your way about like you did in Middlemarsh."

All day long Barney and Bea worked to tidy up the burrow. Bea and Baxter washed and waxed it and cleaned and swept it while Barney and Boris made beds and chairs and a table where the whole family could sit and share a meal. They painted a sign for the door: *BROWN HOUSE.* "Because it is brown inside and because we are the Brown rabbits."

But during that long wet journey, Barney had caught a chill. By midday all he could do was crawl into bed and sleep. Mrs Brown sat down beside him to rest, with Baxter and Boris at her feet. They only meant to rest for a moment. But they were worn out with all their work, and soon fell fast asleep in their clean and cosy new home.

Barney caught a chill

"Shshsh. They are all asleep. We must play quietly," said Blondie.

"Shshsh. Pa's not well. We must play farther from the house," said Billie.

"Let's catch fairies!" cried Bud.

Thistledown

Now this was a favourite game of the little Brown rabbits. They loved to pretend that the tufts of thistledown floating on the breeze were fairies. And they chased them here and there, high and low, trying to biff them with their paws.

A sharp spring wind was blowing a cloud of thistledown through the wood, and the little rabbits ran this way and that, leaping and biffing and chasing the airy fluff. They were having a wonderful time until Bud, the smallest rabbit, fell head-over-heels into a deep, splashy ditch.

"Oh help! Get me out!" cried Bud.

Together they pulled Bud out

Blondie and Billie came running. But the ditch was too deep and the sides were too steep. They did not know how to get Bud out. "Don't worry, youngest! We'll go and get Pa!" they cried, and away they ran in the direction of Brown House.

At least they *thought* it was in the direction of Brown House.

But during their game, they had run a long, long way down many strange paths. In Middlemarsh they knew every tree, every path, every bush, every stone. But here nothing looked familiar. In short, they could not find their way back to Brown House. They were quite, quite lost.

Luckily, they happened to meet a friendly frog who was sitting by a large stone sheltering from the wind. "Oh please help us!" they cried. "Our little brother has fallen into a ditch and we can't get him out!"

The frog came to the rescue, and together they pulled Bud out of the splashy ditch.

"I don't believe I have had the pleasure of meeting you before," said the frog. He bowed deeply. "Let me introduce myself. I am Mr Oggie the Frog-og. And I live in Pease Pond, under those oak trees over there."

"We live in a lovely, big, dry, cosy burrow called Brown House," said Blondie, "but we can't find it *anywhere* because we wandered too far, too soon. You see, we only arrived here from Middlemarsh this morning. My name is Blondie . . ."

". . . and I'm Billie."

". . . and I'm Bud – *atchoo!*"

"Dear me," said Oggie. "We must certainly help you find your way home. It is not quite safe for such small rabbits to be out alone in the Big World. There are *dangers*, you know. But before we begin to search, allow me to welcome you to your new country, one and all." He bowed low again. "Welcome to Brambledown Wood. I hope you will be very happy living here."

"*Where* did you say?" asked Billie.

"Why Brambledown, of course! The best corner in the whole round world," said Oggie.

"Do you mean to say that we *have* come to live in Brambledown, after all?" said Blondie, clapping her paws with delight. "It is famous far and wide!"

Oggie looked pleased. "Oh life isn't perfect here. We have our wicked Weasles and the fiendish Mr Fox. And Farmer Hayseed gets angry when we go shopping in his vegetable garden. We have our squabbles and our sulks, our bullies and our bad-guys. But all in all you won't find a better place to live . . . all supposing you *can* find where you live, I mean . . . Look out! What did I say? Here comes a danger and a half!"

"Look out!"

It was the fiendish Mr Fox

Chapter Three

FRIENDS AND FOES

Quickly the three little rabbits hid behind a tree. They were only just in time. For who should come by but the fiendish Mr Fox? He had a kind of a grin on his furry face, and sang as he went:

"A-hunting I will go,
A-hunting I will go!
Eee aye addio,
A-hunting I will go!

A rabbit for my tea,
A rabbit, maybe three!
Eee aye addio,
A rabbit for my tea!"

Blondie and Billie and Bud dared not even breathe, for the fox might hear them and think about his tea.

"Oh, I wish I were back home in Middlemarsh with only the trains to make me shake!" said Blondie, trembling from head to foot after Mr Fox had gone.

"Now, now," said Oggie the Frog. "Don't talk like that. You live in Brambledown now and Brambledown will look after you. You'll see. Come with me and we'll ask around. Somebody is bound to know this big, dry, cosy burrow. Then they can show you home."

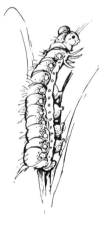

"Shan't, won't"

The first person they met was Claud Caterpillar. "I've never seen anyone as ugly or green as you before," said Blondie. "Please tell us, if you know, where there is a big, dry, cosy rabbit burrow under a tall elm tree!" But Claud was so offended that he only bristled the long spines on his green back and went on his way saying, "Shan't, won't."

"Perhaps if you were more po-polite," said Oggie the Frog, "people might help."

"I only said he was ugly and green," said Blondie in astonishment.

"How would you like it if someone called you ug-ugly and brown?" said Oggie.

"But I'm *not* ugly!"

"I expect Claud Caterpillar thinks you are. Besides, Claud will change into a butterfly one day – more beautiful than any rude young rabbit."

So when they met the Crane Fly, Blondie said, "Excuse me, handsome Mr Crane Fly, sir. I never saw such lovely long legs in my life. Please tell us, if you know, where there is a big, dry, cosy burrow at the foot of a tall elm tree."

"I don't know. But I'll look, if you like," said Mr Crane Fly.

"I'll look if you like"

Oggie hopped away to his pond to ask the fishes and the snails if they knew the way to Brown House. The Crane Fly flew away to look for the big, dry, cosy burrow. When they met anyone on their way, they spread the news of the lost little rabbits and of the new family living in Brambledown Wood. The Crane Fly told the Dragonfly, the Dragonfly told the Woodpecker, and the Woodpecker told the Blackbird and the Blackbird told the Cockerel and the Cockerel trumpeted the news aloud from the roof of the barn.

Little lost rabbits

The three little lost rabbits heard the chatter in the tree-tops, the whispering in the long grass, the whistling in the bushes, but they did not realize that all Brambledown was out searching. They felt lost and alone and very, very hungry.

Mr Wise-Owl heard it from the Cockerel, and he told the Jay. The Jay, of course, told *everyone*. The Grass-Snake told Maurice the Mole, and Maurice Mole told Henry Hedge-hog who passed it on to the Squirrels.

Jay told *everyone*

Of course, word reached the fiendish Mr Fox and the wicked Weasels, which was a very bad thing, because they went out looking for the little lost rabbits, to eat them up.

The Beetles told each other

The Black-back Bee-tles told each other, and someone even climbed up the hill to tell Hoppity Hare. Meanwhile, Mrs Brown woke up and called to her youngest children. "Blondie! Billie! Bud! Come inside now!"

They were lost deep in the wood

Chapter Four

FOUND!

"Where are you, Blondie? Where are you, Billie? Where are you, Bud?"

The sun was going down, Mrs Brown called and called, as loudly as her soft brown voice would allow, into the darkening forest, but there was no answer. "I hope you're not hiding from me. I'll be angry if you are!" But no little rabbits came bounding out from behind the trees. Mrs Brown got her husband out of bed. "Oh Barney! I told them not to go far. They don't know these woods, and now they are lost and it's getting dark! I'm really getting worried."

So Barney started to call, too. "Blondie! Billie! Bud! Come at once!" he said through the cold in his nose. But the little rabbits could not hear. They were lost deep in the wood.

The keen-eyed moth

Blondie, Billie and Bud had decided to hold paws and stay in one place until help arrived.

They were curled up, all three together. It was easier to be brave like that. But as the evening got gloomier and gloomier, it got harder and harder to be brave. Their six little ears trembled like flower petals.

A keen-eyed moth flew over and peered down at them, but then she fluttered on her way, because she had never seen these three little strangers before in the village of Brambledown.

Soon the daylight was gone completely and it was very dark. The sky above the branches was navy blue, and dark shapes swooped about. The little rabbits had never been out at night, even in Middlemarsh. They had never seen the stars' cold glitter. They had never tasted the cold night air.

They had never seen an owl before, or even heard its eerie hooting and shrieking. They had never heard the toads croaking at night, or the rustle of hedgehogs rootling for worms.

Never seen an owl...

They had never seen a colony of bats steering by the stars, flying across the large, white face of the moon.

"I wish we were back in Middlemarsh, squashed up in the leaky, little burrow where

... or a colony of bats

we were born," said Blondie. But she thought of what the Frog said and tried to be brave.

"What's that noise? I think it's coming this way!"

"Shall we run?" asked Bud.

"Shall we hide?" said Billie.

"Perhaps it's Mr Fox coming back," thought Blondie.

"What's all that whispering and whimpering I can hear with my magic ears?" said a gruff voice, and two big boots came tramping into view. The light from a lantern made a big yellow pool on the ground. The owner of the lantern wore a pointy little hat and a pointy little beard and pointy little tails to his coat. His lamp dazzled the little rabbits and they put their paws over their eyes. "Aha! I spy strangers in Brambledown Wood! And what are they doing out at this time of night? Perhaps they're *burglars*!"

"No! No! No!" cried Blondie leaping up. "We're not! We are lost little rabbits!"

"Then you'd best come home with me!" he said and led them back to his cottage.

"You'd best come home with me!"

Goodness the Garden Gnome put back his head and laughed for all he was worth.

"How frightened you looked!" he chortled as he served them milk and cookies. "Anyone would think I was a great grisly ogre coming to eat you up!"

The little lost rabbits laughed too, now that they were safe and warm in the kind Gnome's little cottage. He made them so welcome. He lit a blazing fire. He drew the curtains tight shut. He cooked them hot buttered toast and he asked them all about themselves.

Blondie explained about the trains and the rain and about the road across Marsh Meadow. And Billie explained about playing till suppertime and chasing thistledown and straying too far from Brown House.

A butterfly called

"And now we're lost!" said Bud.

"Not for long, I hope!" said Goodness the Gnome.

Next day a butterfly came to the door. "We have all been searching for the rabbits' new home and the Bee thinks she has seen it. Does it have a green door and a sign outside saying *BROWN HOUSE*?"

"Bee knows"

"Oh yes, yes, yes, yes!" cried the little rabbits. "Oh *thank you*, beautiful butterfly!"

"That's all right," said the Butterfly. "I felt sorry for you even though you did call me an ugly green thing."

"Oh! Are you Claud Caterpillar? But you're more beautiful than anyone in the whole forest now – except for Ma and Pa, of course," said Blondie.

Claud Butterfly looked extremely pleased. "I can see that getting lost has improved your manners, young rabbit." He explained where Brown House was, and then Goodness and the three little rabbits set off to find it.

"All safe home again"

Barney and Bea Brown ran up and down the forest paths calling for their little lost children. Baxter and Boris searched, too. They had not slept a wink all night, and they were wild with worry.

Then a bee buzzed by and said, "Have you lost three young rabbits, by any chance? Ah, then you must be the Browns. Welcome."

Then a hare came bounding past. "Oh you must be the Browns. Welcome. Welcome."

A hedgehog and a mole put their heads out of their holes. "Ah! You must be the Brown rabbits. Welcome!"

Mrs Brown begged them, "Do you know where my babies are?"

"Coming, coming," cooed a pigeon as it flew over. "Don't fret. Don't fret. Go home and wait for them there."

And after breakfast Goodness the Gnome arrived, with Blondie and Billie and Bud. "All safe home again," he said as the family hugged and kissed one another.

Of course Blondie wanted to tell all about their adventures: ". . . how Bud fell into a ditch and then we met Mr Oggie the Frog and then we hid from Mr Fox . . ."

But Mrs Brown put her paw to her lips. "Hush, dear. I want to thank Mr Goodness for bringing you home. However did you find us, sir? The burrow is so well hidden and we only came here yesterday!"

"Oho, nothing stays a secret for long in Brambledown," said Goodness with a giggle.

"Yes, Pa! Do you hear?" cried Blondie. "We *have* come to live in Brambledown after all. I bet you knew all along. I bet you knew exactly how to find Brambledown!"

Well Barney tried to look wise and clever and stared at the sky and stroked one ear and said, "Perhaps."

Mrs Brown looked fondly at her three littlest rabbits. There were leaves in their ears and mud in their fur and toast crumbs in their whiskers.

"I think it's time I did some washing," she said.

"Yes indeed," said Goodness the Gnome. "You will all want to look your best for the party later today."

"What party?" said Mrs Brown with a start.

"Why the *house-warming*, of course!"

"Time I did some washing"

Very welcome indeed

Chapter Five

THE HOUSE-WARMING

You see, there is a tradition in Brambledown. Whenever somebody new comes to live in the district, everyone pays a visit to introduce themselves and to say 'welcome'.

The idea of a party threw Mrs Brown into a panic. But Goodness the Garden Gnome said, "Don't worry about cooking. Everybody will bring a little something to eat and drink, and I'll play some music for the dancing."

Sure enough, before noon animals from all over Brambledown began to arrive. Oggie the Frog and Hoppity Hare, Henry Hedgehog and Maurice Mole – all the birds and insects and squirrels and snakes . . . each of them carrying a pot or a pan or a jug or a jar with something delicious in it, and they made the Browns very welcome indeed!

I'm glad to say that none of the wicked Weasels or the fiendish Mr Fox found their way to BROWN HOUSE for the party.

Goodness the Gnome played his fiddle and everybody danced. The animals twirled and whirled until they were too exhausted to dance any more.

Some of the guests brought food and some brought drink. But some brought little presents for the house – a pine cone or a bunch of pretty feathers. Some offered to help Barney with any repairs he needed to do. And some offered to mind Mrs Brown's *big* family if she wanted to go out.

"Now I know why Brambledown is famous far and wide," said Barney laughing out loud. "It's the best place in the world to live because it has such kind people living here already!"

"My door will always be open to you, my dear friends," said Mrs Brown.

"Don't let Mr Fox hear you," said Goodness, and struck up another tune.

All the Brambledown creatures wanted to hear about Middlemarsh. They shivered when they heard about the rain-leaky burrow. They wailed when they heard about the town people building a road over Marsh Meadow and driving out all the little animals. But they did not understand about the trains, because they had never seen a railway train, never felt one shake the earth as it rushed by spitting smoke into the country air.

"And worst of all," said Mrs Brown, "there was no school in Middlemarsh."

"Oh I didn't mind that," said Blondie.

"Nor me," said Billie.

"Nor me," said Bud. "I hope there isn't one here, either!"

"Oh but there is," said Sabrina Squirrel. "And I'm the school-teacher.

"I'm the teacher"

"What, not learn to jump?"

"I shall expect to see you at school on Monday morning, for counting and reading."

You never saw three faces fall so far. "Oh do we *have* to, Ma?" said Blondie.

"Do we *have* to, Pa," said Billie and Bud.

"What! Not to learn how to jump?" said Oggie the Frog.

"What! Not learn how to run?" said Mrs Mouse.

"What! Not learn how to dig?" said Maurice Mole.

"What! Not learn how to find your way in the Wood?" said the Jay.

"What! Not learn how to play the fiddle and dance?" said Goodness the Gnome ". . . and how to make *toast*?"

"But that sounds like *fun*," said Blondie.

"And why shouldn't school be fun?" asked Sabrina Squirrel. "School in Brambledown is the greatest fun in the world."

"Can I go to school, too?" said Baxter.

"And me?" said Boris.

"I wouldn't mind going myself," said Barney Brown, "if I were a bit younger. Tell me. Does anyone know who lived in this burrow before we got here? It's such a fine, dry, cosy burrow. Who would leave it empty? Who would leave Brambledown?"

Henry spoke up

The creatures looked at one another, but no-one seemed to know until Henry Hedgehog spoke up. "I remember – a long time ago – a rabbit called Rufus.

Some of the old animals nodded their heads and said, "Ah! Rufus! Now I remember."

"Rufus loved adventure," Henry went on. "He said that Brambledown was dull and dreary, boring and ordinary. He packed a bag and away he went to look for adventure. He said, 'I shall be the greatest rabbit in the history of the world, and when I come back you will want me to be King of Brambledown because I am so famous – such a star among rabbits!'"

"What became of him?" asked Mrs Brown.

"Who knows? We never heard."

"I had forgotten all about him," said Maurice Mole.

"So I don't think he became the greatest rabbit in the history of the world," said Barney. "But if he does, and he comes back and wants his house, we will pack up and go, of course. In the meantime, I think I'll make do with Brambledown adventures."

"I don't think I like adventures," said Bud, thinking about the ditch and the Fox and the gloomy, star-pricked night.

One by one, the guests went home and left the Browns alone in their new home.

"I'm going to like it here," said Blondie, as her mother tucked her in.

"Me too," said Billie.

But Bud only snored, because he was already asleep.

When all five children were sleeping, Barney and Bea Brown went outside again and danced by the light of the moon, because they were so happy to have found BROWN HOUSE and Brambledown.

By the light of the moon